D1237825

Princess Charleston of The Isle of Palms

By

Kelly Sheehy DeGroot

Illustrations by

Sara Japanwalla

Published by Tuxedos & Beans in the United States of America 2011
Princess Charleston of the Isle of Palms ISBN 978-0-615-55780-9
Copyright © 2011

This book is dedicated to the original Princess Charleston, my own Prince J, and our beloved T&B. My loves and my inspirations.

Once upon a time there lived a princess named Charleston. She ruled over the land of the Isle of Palms.

One of her duties as the Princess of the Isle of Palms was to protect her friends in the ocean. She protected the dolphins, the sea turtles, the whales, the sharks, and even her friends the seagulls who lived in the air above the water.

Princess Charleston had a magic window in her bedroom. She used her magic window to see all of her ocean friends.

A storm was coming and Princess Charleston wanted to make sure her friends were safe...

But when Princess Charleston looked into her magic window to check on the seagulls she saw that they had nowhere to go.

She sang her magic song, "I wish you nothing but the best, I wish you shelter and good rest. Be safe, be warm, and I will see you in the morn."

And from her song a special seagull house magically appeared under a grand pavilion on the beach. It was filled with seagull beds, seagull toys, and seagull food.

When Princess Charleston checked her window the seagulls were happy and safe in their new shelter as the storm began to rumble high up in the sky.

Then Princess Charleston saw her friend Crabby the Crab in her special window. He was scurrying along the beach looking for a safe place to hide from the storm.

Princess Charleston sang her magical song again, "I wish you nothing but the best, I wish you shelter and good rest. Be safe, be warm, and I will see you in the morn."

And a little hole opened up for Crabby right there on the beach.

"Thank you Princess Charleston," said Crabby as he scurried inside the hole to find crab food and crab toys for him to use as he waited for the storm to pass.

The clouds above the ocean began to get darker and darker and darker, until they were almost black. A flash of lightning streaked through the sky and Princess Charleston heard a loud CRACK! of thunder. Suddenly, the rain began to fall.

Hundreds of big wet droplets began to pound on the ocean ceiling and the water began to push and pull this way and that.

The next morning Princess Charleston took a long walk on the beach to check on her friends the seagulls and Crabby the Crab.

Princess Charleston saw the seagulls come out from underneath the grand pavilion on the beach. They shook the sand off their tails and waved their wings to Princess Charleston. "Princess Charleston," said the seagulls, "thanks to you we were safe and warm under the grand pavilion last night."

The seagulls flew above Princess Charleston as she walked farther down the beach waving to all her friends.

Soon she came across a hole in the sand and Crabby the Crab quickly danced out from within. "Thanks to you Princess Charleston, I was safe and warm under the sand last night," said Crabby.

Princess Charleston smiled and turned to go back home when she noticed that all of her sea friends were gathered in the water and on the sand smiling at her.

"We all want to thank you Princess Charleston for keeping us safe and warm," said all of the creatures. And all at once they began to sing, "We wish you nothing but the best, we wish you shelter and good rest. Be safe, be warm, and we will see you in the morn."

The End